Take Care, Good Knight

Shelley Moore Thomas ◆ PICTURES BY **Paul Meisel**

Dutton Children's Books

For Noel
—S.M.T.

For my "little" dragons,
Peter, Alex, and Andrew
—P.M.

DUTTON CHILDREN'S BOOKS
A division of Penguin Young Readers Group

Published by the Penguin Group
Penguin Group (USA) Inc., 375 Hudson Street, New York, New York 10014, U.S.A.
Penguin Group (Canada), 90 Eglinton Avenue East, Suite 700, Toronto, Ontario, Canada M4P 2Y3 (a division
of Pearson Penguin Canada Inc.) • Penguin Books Ltd, 80 Strand, London WC2R 0RL, England • Penguin Ireland,
25 St Stephen's Green, Dublin 2, Ireland (a division of Penguin Books Ltd) • Penguin Group (Australia), 250 Camberwell
Road, Camberwell, Victoria 3124, Australia (a division of Pearson Australia Group Pty Ltd) • Penguin Books India Pvt
Ltd, 11 Community Centre, Panchsheel Park, New Delhi - 110 017, India • Penguin Group (NZ), Cnr Airborne and
Rosedale Roads, Albany, Auckland 1310, New Zealand (a division of Pearson New Zealand Ltd) • Penguin Books
(South Africa) (Pty) Ltd, 24 Sturdee Avenue, Rosebank, Johannesburg 2196, South Africa
Penguin Books Ltd, Registered Offices: 80 Strand, London WC2R 0RL, England

Library of Congress Cataloging-in-Publication Data

Thomas, Shelley Moore.
Take care, Good Knight / by Shelley Moore Thomas; pictures by Paul Meisel.—1st ed.
p. cm
Summary: The three little dragons have agreed to take care of the old wizard's cats
while he is away, but their inability to read his instructions causes problems until
their friend, the Good Knight, saves the day.
Special Markets ISBN 978-0-525-47927-7 Not for Resale
[1. Dragons—Fiction. 2. Knights and knighthood—Fiction. 3. Cats—Fiction.
4. Literacy—Fiction.] I. Meisel, Paul, ill. II. Title.
PZ7.T369453Tak 2006 [E]—dc22 2005036722

Published in the United States by Dutton Children's Books,
a division of Penguin Young Readers Group
345 Hudson Street, New York, New York 10014
www.penguin.com/youngreaders
Designed by Sara Reynolds and Abby Kuperstock
Manufactured in China
5 7 9 10 8 6 4

Once there were three little dragons. The dragons lived in a deep dark cave that was in the king's forest. But the dragons were very happy in their cave.

They had a good friend. He was called the Good Knight.
Every day he rode his horse—clippety-clop, clippety-clop—to the
dragons' cave to say, "Good morning, good dragons."

"Good morning, Good Knight," replied the dragons.

And every night he rode his horse—clippety-clop, clippety-clop—to put the little dragons to bed.

"Good night, Good Knight," the dragons said before they went to sleep.

One day, after the Good Knight had ridden off on his horse—clippety-clop—the little dragons heard a knock on the door. It was another friend, the old, old wizard.

"Good day, little dragons. I was wondering if you could help me," the old, old wizard said.

"We will try," said the dragons.

"I would like you to watch my cats while I go away for a few days. Can you do it?"

The dragons had never watched cats before. But the Good Knight had taught them that it was good to do good deeds.

"Certainly, we will help you," said the dragons.

The old, old wizard was very happy. He told the dragons that he would leave a note with instructions at his cottage. He left them the shiny silver key to his door. "Take care, good dragons," he said. And then he disappeared in a puff of smoke.

"This is going to be fun!"
said the first dragon.

"I can hardly wait,"
said the second dragon.

"Yippee!"
said the third dragon.

The next day the dragons went to the wizard's cottage to take care of the cats. They opened the door with the shiny silver key. They saw lots of cats.

They found the wizard's note on the counter. There was only one problem. The dragons didn't know how to read!

Give the cats fresh water.

Give the cats food from the cupboard.

Put the cats to sleep in their beds at night.

"I think the first thing we're supposed to do is take the cats swimming in the lake," said the first dragon.

So the dragons gathered up the cats and took them to the lake for a swim.

Just then, the Good Knight was riding by on his horse.

"Good day, good dragons," said the Good Knight. "What are you doing?"

"We are taking the wizard's cats for a swim," said the dragons. "He told us to."

Cats swimming? That did not seem right. But if the old wizard said so, it must be true. "Very well," said the Good Knight. "Carry on."

But the cats did not like swimming. They did not like it one bit. They howled and yowled. They quivered and shivered until . . .

. . . the little dragons took them home.

Then the little dragons looked at the wizard's note to see
what to do next.

"I think it says to put the cats in the cupboard," said the
second dragon.

CAT
FOOD

CAT
FOOD

So the dragons put the cats in the cupboard.

Just then, the Good Knight was riding by. "What are you doing?" asked the Good Knight.

"We are putting the wizard's cats in the cupboard. He told us to."

Cats in the cupboard? That did not seem right. But if the old wizard said so, it must be true. "Very well," said the Good Knight. "Carry on."

But the cats did not like being in the cupboard. They did not like it one bit. They scritched and scratched until the little dragons let them out.

By then the cats were very thirsty and very hungry. And so were the little dragons. But they looked at the note once more. "I think now we are supposed to take the cats camping," said the third dragon.

So the dragons took the cats out camping under the stars.

"What are you doing?" asked the Good Knight, who was coming to bring the dragons back to their cave.

"We are taking the cats out camping," said the dragons. "The old wizard told us to."

Cats camping? That did not seem right. But if the wizard said so, it must be true. "Very well," said the Good Knight. "Carry on."

But the cats didn't like camping. They didn't like it one bit.
They jumped and bumped. They clawed and pawed. They
cussed and fussed and hissed! And they would not even eat one
toasted marshmallow.

The Good Knight could not help but hear all the racket the cats were making. *Something doesn't seem right!* he thought.

Back he rode to the wizard's house—clippety-clop.

"Follow me, good dragons," he said. "Let us get to the bottom of this. And bring those cats!"

Inside the wizard's house, the Good Knight found the wizard's note. It did not say to take the cats swimming. It did not say to put the cats in the cupboard or to take them camping. "Didn't you read this note?" he asked.

The dragons hung their heads. Their eyes filled with drippy droppy tears. "We told him we would take care. But we don't know how to read," they confessed.

So the Good Knight read the note to the dragons.

First they gave
the cats water.

Then they fed the cats
food from the cupboard.

And they put the cats
in their beds to sleep.

By then the dragons were very tired themselves. The Good Knight walked them back to their cave and tucked them in for the night.

The next day, the wizard came back from his trip. He
visited the dragons. "Thank you for watching my cats," he said.
"You did such a good job, I wanted you to have this." He
handed them a tiny baby kitten of their own.

"And I wanted you to have this," said the Good Knight. He handed a book to the dragons.

It was a book about learning to read!